THE DETECTIVE FRIENDS Series

MYSTERY STORIES FOR KIDS

by: Unity B.

This Book Belongs to: Millie 6TP

Contact No:

Unity B and UJB publications assert the moral right to be identified as the authors of this book.

First edition July 2023

Written by: Unity B

Book Design & published by: UJB Publications

www.ujbbooks.com

DISCLAIMER

"The Detective Friends- Mystery Stories for kids" is a work of fiction. Any resemblance to actual persons, living or dead, or actual events is purely coincidental. The characters, incidents, and dialogues in this storybook are products of the author's imagination and are not to be construed as real.

While the stories may involve mysteries and detective work, they are intended purely for entertainment purposes and should not be taken as real-life investigative methods or procedures. The author, Unity B, has crafted an imaginative world with colorful characters and exciting adventures to engage young readers.

Parents and guardians are encouraged to read the book with their children and discuss the distinction between fiction and reality. It is important to remind young readers that the activities, decisions, and outcomes in the stories are fictional and should not be replicated in real-life situations without proper guidance and supervision.

"The Detective Friends- Mystery Stories for kids" aims to inspire imagination, critical thinking, and problem-solving skills in young readers. It is a work of literary creation and should be enjoyed as such.

Remember, the world of fiction offers a safe and exciting escape, where imaginations can soar. Enjoy the adventures of four friends "The Detective Friends- Mystery stories for kids" while understanding the boundaries of fiction and reality.

TABLE OF CONTENTS

Hey ! I am max
I love eating S'more

She is my friend Olivia
She is so intelligent..

He is Leo,
our funniest friend.

And She is our friend
Lily who is always little
scared.

PREAMBLE

This book is about four little friends, Max, Olivia, Leo, and Lily who used to study together at Elmwood Elementary School.

Max, was a foodie who was known for his insatiable appetite and his love for all things culinary. He often used to carry a bag of snacks wherever he went.

Olivia was an intelligent girl who had a thirst for knowledge. She was always engrossed in books, and eager to learn something new.

Leo was the funniest of all and was the epitome of humour and joviality. Leo would often crack jokes even in the most serious conditions as he was always lighthearted and never took things seriously.

Lily, on the other hand, was a little scared and timid by nature. She was always on edge, easily startled by the smallest of noises or unexpected surprises. Despite her fearful demeanour, Lily had an uncanny ability to notice the tiniest details that often went unnoticed by others.

They were all excited as they were all going to the summer camp, where they would soon discover their hidden talents and their strengths as a team.

1. The Mystery at Summer Camp

The sun was shining brightly as a group of excited kids arrived at Camp Adventure, ready for an unforgettable summer camp experience.

Four little friends, Max, Olivia, Leo, and Lily couldn't contain their excitement as they stepped onto the campgrounds.

Chapter 1: The Strange Happenings

Max: (Wide-eyed) "Camp Adventure, here we come! I can practically taste the S'mores already. My taste buds are ready for a wild adventure!"

Olivia: (With an eager grin) "And just think of all the new skills and knowledge we'll gain in the great outdoors. I'm ready to explore and learn!"

Leo: (Playfully) "Oh, I can't wait to see what kind of mischievous adventures we'll find ourselves in. I hope there's a secret tunnel somewhere!"

Lily: (Nervously) "Um, guys, did you hear that strange noise coming from the woods last night? It gave me goosebumps. I hope it's not haunted!"
"Shut up Lily and stop getting scared", said Olivia.

"True. We are here for fun and excitement so let us begin our journey by tasting some S'mores. My stomach is craving for some food now", said Max.

The kids laughed and started having some tasty food prepared for them.

Little did they know, this summer camp had more in store for them than they could ever imagine.

Everything seemed perfect until peculiar things started happening.

Supplies went missing, spooky noises echoed through the woods at night, and strange footprints appeared near the cabins.

Chapter 2: Uncovering Clues

Everyone at the camp was scared and confused with these mysterious happenings.

Undeterred by these happening, Max, Olivia, Leo, and Lily decided to form their own detective club, determined to uncover the truth behind the strange occurrences at Camp Adventure.

Max: (Putting on a detective hat) "Ladies and gentlemen, we are facing a mystery which we need to solve."

"Someone has tried to mess up with my tasty food, and so I need to find the culprit and restore the food supply."

Olivia: "True, together we are extraordinary detectives of Camp! Together, we'll solve the mysteries that others can't."

Further on examining footprints, "Look at these footprints near the cabins. They're unlike any ordinary camper's footprints. Someone with an extraordinary sense of fashion must have left them!"

Leo: (With a mischievous smirk) "Maybe it's not a person at all! Perhaps it's a gang of stealthy squirrels who are tired of eating acorns and have turned to a life of camp pranks!"

Lily: (Nervously) "Or... maybe it's the ghost of a fashion-forward camper who couldn't resist leaving their stylish mark on the campgrounds. The ghost of Camp Fashionista!"

"Will you both please stop and help us investigate this issue?" Olivia asked Leo and Lily as she began to examine the strange footsteps.

Chapter 3: Nighttime Adventures

Determined to solve the mystery, the detective club embarked on a thrilling nighttime adventure, ready to uncover the truth behind the strange happenings. Armed with flashlights and a notepad, they hid near the cabins, waiting for any suspicious activity.

Max: (Whispering) "Tonight, under the cover of darkness, we embark on a mission of epic proportions! Like silent shadows, we shall reveal the secrets that lurk in the night."

"I am anxious to catch the one who came between me and my food!"

Olivia: (Quietly observing) "Look over there! I see a shadowy figure sneaking around one of the cabins."

We must follow them discreetly and discover their secrets.

Leo: (whispering with excitement) "This is like being characters in a thrilling spy movie! We're on the verge of a breakthrough, my fellow detectives. Let's catch them red-handed!"

Lily: (whispering nervously) "Please, no unexpected encounters with friendly ghosts or prankster raccoons. My heart can't handle any more surprises!"

"Shut up Lily!" said Olivia again, who started following the shadowy figure.

Chapter 4: Solving the Mystery

As the detective club followed the shadowy figure, it led them deep into the woods, where they discovered a hidden cabin filled with stolen camp supplies.

Max: (In awe) "Behold, the secret hideout of thievery! This is where all the missing supplies have been stashed. We're getting closer to cracking this case!"

Olivia: (Reading from a journal) "Look, it's Mr. Johnson's journal!"

"It contains detailed plans to scare everyone away from the camp and claim the land for himself."

"He's the culprit!"

Armed with evidence, the Detective Club confronted Mr. Johnson. He confessed his scheme.

The kids alerted the camp director, who took immediate action, ensuring the safety of the camp and the well-being of the campers.

Leo: (In a heroic tone) "We've solved the mystery!"

"The camp is safe once again, thanks to the extraordinary Detective Club. We're like superheroes, but we don't wear capes, just cool detective hats!"

Lily: (Relieved) "Finally, the camp can return to its joyful and ghost-free state. Our mission is complete, my fearless friends."

Max: (With a mischievous grin) "And let's not forget the amazing adventures and laughs we had along the way! Who knew detective work could be this fun?"

Olivia: (Reflectively) "We've not only solved the mystery but also discovered the power of friendship and teamwork. Together, we can conquer any challenge."

Leo: (Jokingly) "And we've proven that even the most mysterious and spooky situations can't dampen our spirits. Camp Adventure won't be the same without us!"

Together: (Celebrating) "The Detective Club triumphs once again! Camp Adventure will forever remember our epic tale of friendship, hilarity, and the most extraordinary summer camp mystery ever solved!"

As the sun set on Camp Adventure, the Detective Club's remarkable adventure came to an end.

Their bond grew stronger, and the memories they created would last a lifetime.

Little did they know that more mysteries and thrilling escapades awaited them in the future..

The four friends walked off into the sunset, ready to face whatever mysteries lay ahead, armed with their humor, friendship, and detective skills.

And so, the legend of the extraordinary Detective Club at Camp Adventure began, inspiring future campers to embrace their curiosity, solve mysteries, and create unforgettable summer camp memories.

 THE END

2. The Mystery of the Missing Pet

Chapter 1: A Pet Friend Goes Missing

In the cosy neighbourhood of Maplewood, where the scent of freshly baked cookies wafted through the air, Lily woke up one morning to find her beloved pet dog, Coco, missing from its hutch.

Panic washed over her as she realized her furry friend had vanished without a trace.

Distraught and worried, Lily immediately called her friends to help her find Coco.

Max, Olivia, and Leo, who happened to live nearby, rushed over to support Lily in her time of need.

Max: (Putting on his detective hat) "Fear not, Lily! The Detective Friends are here to help you. We'll find Coco in no time!"

Olivia: (Analyzing the situation) "Let's start by interviewing the neighbors and searching every nook and cranny. Coco couldn't have gone far."

Leo: (Gently patting Lily's back) "Don't worry. We'll bring Coco back safe and sound. Remember how we solved the Camp Mystery case?"

"We are together a strong team and we will crack this case soon."

Chapter 2:
Investigating the Neighbourhood

The Pet Detective Club began their investigation by interviewing neighbors and searching the neighborhood for any signs of Coco.

They knocked on doors, put up posters, and talked to anyone who might have seen or heard something unusual.

They also kept a lookout for any mysterious clues.

The Detective friends donned their detective gear and set out to investigate the neighbourhood, determined to uncover any clues that could lead them to Coco.

Max: (Ringing doorbells) "Excuse me, Ma'am, have you seen a dog running around lately? We're on a mission to find our friend Coco."

"No my dear", said Mrs Anderson who lived nearby.

"Thank you", said Max. He pulled out his favorite S'mores from his bag and as he started eating it.

He knocked on the door of the next neighbor, "Excuse me, Sir, have you seen a dog nearby lately? We are trying to locate our dog, Coco".

Mr.Thompson (nervously trying to avoid eye contact),

"Coco? No... I don't think so that I saw Coco recently."

"No problem Sir. Thank you", said Max.

Olivia: (Hanging up "Missing Dog" posters) Keep an eye out, everyone! Coco might have left a trail or someone might have spotted her in their backyard.

Leo: (Whispering to the team) "Look, there's Mr. Thompson. He seems nervous whenever we approach him. Let's keep a close watch on him."

Lily: (nervously) "I am very scared guys!"

Leo: (cracking a joke) "Don't worry Lily. By the way don't you think we are doing the reverse? In the movies, it is generally the dog who sniffs around and takes us to the criminal, but here it is us who are sniffing around trying to locate the criminal!"

Olivia: (consoling Lily) "Leo please it is not funny. Lily is missing her Coco. Don't worry we will crack this case for sure."

The detective friends decided to keep a close watch on him, believing he might be hiding something.

Chapter 3: The Hidden Hideout

That afternoon, as the Detective friends discreetly followed Mr.Thompson, they noticed him entering an old shed at the back of his property. Their curiosity was piqued; they couldn't resist taking a peek inside.

Max: (Whispering) "Shh! Look, it's Coco!
He is hopping happily around the shed."

Olivia: (With a gasp) "So, Mr. Thompson
has been hiding Coco all along?
But why?"

Leo: (Scratching his head) "This is
turning out to be a peculiar mystery."

"Let's rescue Coco and find out what
Mr.Thompson's up to."

Lily (with great relief) "Thank God, I
can see Coco again. For a moment I
thought I have lost him forever."

Chapter 4: Unravelling the Mystery

Confused and excited, the Pet Detective Club took Coco back to Lily's house. They gathered all the evidence.

It soon became clear that Mr.Thompson had accidentally let Coco out of her hutch and had been secretly taking care of her in the shed.

Soon Mr. Thomson left that place for some work and detective friends entered the old shed and took custody of Coco.

With Coco safely in their arms, the Detective friends returned to Lily's house, eager to piece together the puzzle they had stumbled upon.

Olivia: (Sorting through the evidence) "It seems Mr.Thompson accidentally let Coco out of the hutch and had been secretly taking care of Coco in his old shed."

Leo: (with a mischievous smile) "Ah, this is a case of pet miscommunication!"

Max: (while eating his favorite S'mores) "We need to confront Mr Thompson and get to the bottom of this."

That evening when Mr Thomson returned from work, they marched to Mr Thompson's house, ready to confront him and solve the mystery.

The Detective Friends: (Knocking on the door) "Mr.Thompson, we know your secret! It's time to come out and explain why you were hiding Coco with you."

Mr.Thompson opened the door, his eyes filled with guilt and remorse.

Mr.Thompson: (Sighing) "I'm sorry, Lily. I accidentally let Coco out, and I was too scared to admit my mistake. I didn't want you to be upset."

"I love Coco very much and I was having a fun time with him."

Lily: (With a mixture of relief and forgiveness) "It's okay, Mr.Thompson. Thank you for taking care of Coco. Just remember to let us know next time, alright?"

Chapter 5: A Joyful Reunion

Lily's heart filled with joy as Coco hopped into her arms, wiggling her fluffy nose with excitement. The Detective friends shared a triumphant smile, knowing they had solved The case of the Missing Pet and brought Coco back home.

Lily: (Hugging Coco tightly) "Thank you, friends, for finding my furry friend."

Max: (Grinning proudly) "Guys this is the second time we have solved a mystery. I am so hungry now after this hard work"

Olivia: (Reflecting) "This mystery taught us the importance of communication and forgiveness. We all make mistakes, but it's how we handle them that matters."

Leo: (With a twinkle in his eye) "And let's not forget the thrill of detective work! We may be small, but we've proven that we can solve any mystery that comes our way."

Together, they celebrated their success, their laughter echoing through the neighborhood.

Max: (Playfully) "Who's up for some celebratory ice cream?
My treat!"

Olivia: (Laughing) "Only if you promise not to eat it all before we even get to the ice cream parlour, Max."

Leo: (Teasingly) "And no funny detective disguises this time, Max."
"We want to enjoy our ice cream in peace."

The four Detective friends, with Coco happily hopping beside them, strolled down the streets of Maplewood to visit the ice cream parlour.

Their bond is stronger than ever. They had proven that with teamwork, determination, and a little humour, they could solve any mystery and bring joy back to their beloved neighbourhood.

And so, the legend of the four Detective friends grew, inspiring others to embrace their detective skills and create a community filled with laughter, friendship, and the unconditional love of their furry companions.

──────── ◈◈◈ ──── THE END ──── ◈◈◈ ────────

3. The Mystery of the Disappearing Toys

Chapter 1: The Mystery Unfolds

In the lively town of Brookville, the beloved toy store named "Playland" was struck by a strange series of events.

Toys began mysteriously vanishing from the shelves, leaving the owners and customers puzzled. The owner of the shop Mr Barker was under great stress.

Mr. Barker's son Tony was a good friend of Max, and he knew Max and his team were solving such mystery cases.

So Tony asked his father to call the four Detective friends who can help him solve this case.

Desperate to solve this mystery, Mr. Barker called on the four friends Max, Olivia, Leo and Lily and explained about the strange disappearance of the toys from his shop.

The Detective friends assured Mr Barker to find the culprit and embarked on a mission to catch the toy thief and restore joy to Playland.

[Inside Playland toy store]

Max: (looking at the empty shelf) "Guys, this is unbelievable! The toys have vanished! How can they just disappear?"

Olivia: (puzzled) "I have no idea, Max. It's like they vanished into thin air! We can't let the toy thief get away with this."

We must solve this mystery and bring joy back to Playland!

Max: (grabbing a bite of S'mores) "We need to get to the bottom of this. We can't let Playland lose its magic."

Leo: (mischievously) "Guys I think this could be the work of some grandfather who wants to gift toys to his grandchildren but has run out of money!"

Lily: (determined) "Or could it be evil spirits coming and taking the toys in the night? I am so scared."

Olivia: (angrily) "Shut up Leo this is no time for a joke. You Lily stop associating everything with ghosts!"

Chapter 2:
Investigating & Trailing the Suspects

"Let us start looking for some clues.

I am pretty sure the thief has left

some clues behind for us."

Max: (whispering) "Okay, team, we need

to gather some clues. Let's split up and

interview the store owners, employees,

and anyone who might have seen

something unusual."

Olivia: (nodding) "I'll start by

questioning the store owners for any

surveillance footage."

Leo: "I will question the employees to see if they have noticed any strange activities lately."

Lily: "I will look out for visitors and see if I can find anything strange."

The detective friends began their investigation.

Olivia: (inquired to Mr. Barker) "Is there surveillance footage available?"

Mr. Barker: "We had CCTV, but unfortunately they stopped working a few days ago."

Leo interviewed the employees to find out if they had observed anything suspicious. But no one could come up with a satisfying answer.

Puzzled by the lack of evidence, they decided to dig deeper and look for leads outside the store.

Lily observed that among all the visitors, two visitors looked suspicious.

The first suspect was a lady with a large bag who appeared overly interested in the toy displayed.

The second suspect was a man in a dark hat and trench coat, lurking around the store.

Max: (eating a bite of S'mores) "Ok team let us keep an eye on both suspects. I and Olivia will watch out for the lady. Lily, you go and follow the man."

Lily: (nervously) "I think the man could have some black magical powers. I am scared to go."

Leo: (Patting Lily) "Stop being nervous. I will come with you. Don't worry."

Chapter 3:
Hideout & Cracking the Thief's Code

Max and Olivia followed the lady to her house. But they found that the lady had purchased the toys from the shop to give them to her daughter.

She did not appear to be the culprit.

On the other hand, Leo and Lily followed the man, and that led them to an abandoned warehouse on the outskirts of town.

Leo: (whispering) "Let us peep through the window of the warehouse to see what is hidden inside."

Lily: (scared) "Please be careful. It is very dark inside and ghosts like to live inside dark places."

Leo: (mischievously) "If I find a ghost, I will send it to you."

Lily: (scared) "Oh no please don't do that. Leo, you know how much I am scared of them!"

Leo: (laughing) "Ok. Ok.. Stop worrying you scared one. I am just joking!"

Leo cautiously climbed the window of the warehouse and discovered a hidden room filled with stolen toys.

Leo: "It was the toy thief's secret hideout. Let us go and call our team and we will catch him red-handed with the toys!"

Lily: "True Leo. Let us all uncover the thief."

Chapter 4: Uncovering the Toy Thief

The detective friends gathered at the Playland store and informed Mr. Barker, We have found the hiding place of the toy thief.

Let us go and uncover the thief's identity.

The detective friends led Mr. Barker to the old warehouse where Leo had seen the missing toys.

Mr. Barker: (in a firm voice) "Come out of your hiding. We know that you have stolen the toys from our shop."

The thief: (scared) "Ok I am coming out Please do forgive me!"

As the door of the warehouse opened, they found that it was Mr. Jenkins. Mr. Jenkins was an eccentric inventor.

Max: (firmly) "Mr. Jenkins, why did you resort to stealing toys from Playland?"

Mr Jenkins: (nervously) "I... I couldn't help myself. I was envious of the joy these toys brought to children. I wanted to create the ultimate toy, but I lost sight of what really mattered."

Olivia: (sympathetic) "Mr.Jenkins, there's a better way to share your creativity. Stealing is never the solution."

Leo: (offering a helping hand) "We believe in second chances, Mr Jenkins. Let's find a way for you to showcase your talent without hurting others."

Mr Barker: (consoling Mr Jenkins) "You can make new toys and bring them to me and I will help you in selling them at our shop."

Mr Jenkins: (ashamed) "Thank you for being so kind. I will return all your toys and also bring the new toys, which I have made for you to sell to children."

Lily: (smiling) "Let's return these stolen toys to Playland and make things right."

Chapter 5: Restoring the Toys

[At the special event organized by Playland]

Crowd: (cheering) "Look, the toys are back! The Four Detective friends have saved the Playland!"

Max: (grateful) "We couldn't have done it without the support of our community. Thank you all for standing by us."

Olivia: (proudly) "Remember, solving mysteries is not just about finding the truth. It's about bringing happiness and justice to our community."

Leo: (smiling) "And together, we'll continue to be the Detective Friends, solving mysteries and making our town a better place."

Lily: (smiling) "And we will help everyone in whatever way we can!"

As the crowd erupts in applause, the fame of four friends spread across the community.

THE END

4. The Mystery at Bake Sale

At Elmwood Elementary School, the annual bake sale was a highly anticipated event. The students, teachers, and parents worked hard to bake delicious treats to raise money for a charity.

Chapter 1: Detectives turn Bakers

Max, being a food lover, proposed an idea to his friends, "What if we participate in 'The Great Bake-Off' and use our detective skills to uncover any foul play? We can ensure fair competition for everyone. We should ensure that there are delicious cookies for everyone - including me of course!"

Olivia's eyes sparkled with mischief. "And of course, we'll bake the most irresistible batch of cookies that will make everyone forget about the stolen ones!"

Leo chuckled, picturing the chaos that would ensue.

"Imagine the look on the judges' faces when they taste our cookies and realize they've been out-baked by a group of detectives."

Lily, the voice of reason, nodded in agreement. "But let's not forget our main mission."

"We need to keep an eye out for any signs of cheating or mischief during the competition."

And so, the four detective friends registered for "The Great Bake-Off" as a team, ready to solve the mystery of any stolen recipes, tampered ingredients, or mischievous antics.

Chapter 2: The competition begins

As the day of the competition arrived, the school cafeteria atmosphere turned electric.

The Cookie Detectives, armed with their detective badges and aprons, set up their baking station, surrounded by eager participants and curious onlookers.

The baking frenzy commenced as contestants mixed, stirred, and whisked their way to culinary glory.

The air was filled with the delightful aroma of pastries, cakes, and, of course, the Cookie Detectives' signature cookies.

Amidst the flurry of activity, the squad kept their keen eyes peeled for any suspicious behaviour.

They observed intense glances, secret ingredient exchanges, and even a few moments of misplaced kitchen utensils.

Lily nudged Leo, pointing discreetly towards a competitor who seemed unusually nervous.

"Something doesn't seem right. Let's keep an eye on that baker."

Leo nodded, observing the contestant closely.

As the judging panel made their rounds, tasting each creation, the squad noticed the baker's hands trembling with anxiety.

Olivia whispered: "I have a feeling that baker might be up to something."

Let's discreetly follow their next move.

Chapter 3: The evil contestant

As the teams rushed into the kitchen to gather ingredients, the detective friends set their eyes on the baker behaving mischievously.

They stealthily trailed the baker to a storage area in the kitchen, hidden behind stacks of baking supplies.

Olivia: "I don't think his intentions look good."

Peeking through the shelves, they witnessed the baker switching a jar of sugar with one filled with salt.

Lily: (gasping) "He is sabotaging the competition! We need to act fast."

Leo: "Not when the detective friends are there! We will not let that happen."

Chapter 4: The Evil Baker uncovered

With the evidence in hand, the detective friends rushed to inform the judges of the devious plan. The competition was temporarily paused as the judges rushed to the kitchen and confronted the cheater.

The baker was their schoolmate Alex.

Olivia: "Alex why did you do this?"

Alex: "I am sorry. I am participating in this competition along with my elder sister Mary."

"She has worked very hard to make the cookies. And so I badly wanted to win this competition as I did not want my sister to lose."

Mary: "Alex you have made me look down. I would rather not win the competition, than win by cheating."

The judges noted that Mary had not participated in any evil practices and so they did not disqualify her.

The Cookie Detectives, amidst a mixture of relief and disappointment, returned to their baking station and the competition continued.

Chapter 5: The winners

The bake sale continued, and the annual charity received an overwhelming outpouring of support from the community.

Every team presented their delicious cookies to the judges.

Mary also presented the batch of irresistible cookies to the judges, who marvelled at the perfect texture, flavour, and aroma.

Finally, the judges made their final selection.

"It is time to announce the winners", said Ms Patricia who was one of the judges. "And the winner is.. Any guesses?", said Mr. Nick, who was the second judge.

As the crowd made a few whispers of their favorite team, the judges revealed the secret.

"The winner is Mary, who has made awesome cookies."

"However, she will be the sole recipient of the award as Alex is disqualified from the contest."

"Also, we have a special prize for the detective friend who prevented fraudulent practices and made this competition fair by using their sharp observations and detective skills."

The four detective friends were super excited to win this special prize.

Their efforts to ensure a fair competition had brought the students, teachers, and parents even closer together.

5. The Mystery of Missing Bike

It was a bright sunny day in the neighbourhood of Sunnyville, where Thomas lived. After finishing his breakfast, Thomas set out to visit his secret gathering place to meet his friends.

Chapter 1: The Missing Bicycle

As we went outside to pull out his bicycle, Thomas suddenly screamed in fear, "My bicycle! I had kept it here last night, but it's gone! I can't believe this!"

Thomas realized that someone had stolen his lovely bicycle and so immediately went to see his friend Micheal.

Micheal: (concerned) "What? Your bicycle is missing? That's terrible, Thomas. I know someone who can help us get back your bicycle!"

Micheal had attended the toy restoration event at the Playland store. So she knew about the four detective friends and took Thomas to them. The four detective friends had an emergency meeting to discuss how they can help Thomas.

Olivia: (determined) "Friends, we are having another case to solve. Someone has stolen Thomas's bicycle and we can't let this go. We have to find his bicycle."

Max: (while eating a cookie) "Let us put on our detective hats and crack this case!"

Lily: (supportive) "Don't worry, Thomas. We're here for you. We'll solve this mystery together!"

Leo: (cheering up) "And if we can't find a new one, then Lily will use her pocket money savings and buy you a new one!

Lily: (annoyed) "Shut up Leo, it is no time for jokes."

"Let us all get to work."

The four detective friends started their investigation work.

Chapter 2: Searching for Clues & Suspicion

The detective friends started the investigation by scouring the area around Thomas's house for any signs of his missing bicycle.

Max: (determined) "OK team. Let us look for any clues."

Lily: (examining the surroundings) "I don't see any tire tracks. Did anyone notice anything unusual?"

Olivia: "That looks strange. It means nobody drove the bicycle from here."

Leo: "That means there are only two possibilities:

Either someone picked up the bicycle in their vehicle or the bicycle got some wings and so flew on its own. Wow, how beautiful would a bicycle look with wings! I missed seeing that."

Olivia: (angrily) "Shut up Leo. Stop cracking your jokes. Let us ask some neighbors to see if they know anything."

Max: (questioning the neighbors) "Excuse me, have you seen anything suspicious around Thomas's house?"

Neighbor 1: "Now that you mention it, I saw a person lurking around here yesterday."

Neighbor 2: "Yeah, I noticed a strange van parked nearby. Could be related."

Neighbor 3: "This is happening more often now. Last week two other kids Sam and Emma living two streets from here, also had their bicycles missing."

Max: (determined) "It seems like more than one bike has gone missing. There's definitely something going on."

Olivia: (thoughtfully) "Friends let us examine the places nearby to see if we can find any more pieces of evidence."

Max: "Friends let us split up to investigate. I and Olivia will go towards the North side and Leo and Lily can go towards the South Side."

Max and Olivia started searching on the North side. After covering ample distance, they entered the woods.

As they continued looking for things in the woods, they stumbled upon a hidden spot in the woods—an old abandoned shed that seemed to be the perfect hideout for a thief.

Leo and Lily went down the South. They also met Sam and Emma and inquired about their missing bicycles. Both of them did have any tyre marks from the missing bicycles.

Lily: (analyzing the situation) "It looks like there is a pattern, and all bicycles might be stolen by the same thief!"

Leo: (confirming) "True, it looks like someone is troubling the innocent children here and we must find that thief."

Chapter 3: The Bike Thief Revealed

After questioning Sam and Emma, Leo and Lily went back to Max and Olivia.

The detective friends cautiously entered the shed, to look out for more clues.

Max: (entering the abandoned shed) "Whoa, look at all these stolen bicycles! We're onto something."

Olivia: (excitedly) "Yes, one of these should be Thomas's bicycle. But why would someone pile up the bicycles here?"

Lily: (inspecting the shed) "Look here. I found something!"

Leo: (inspecting the object) "It looks like a diary. It has a list of addresses."

Max: (reading the diary) "Wait, the third address is Thomas's address."

Lily: (reading the diary) "The first and second addresses are Sam and Emma's addresses!"

Olivia: (decoding the puzzle) "So if I am not wrong the fourth address is the address where the thief will steal."

Max: (confirming) "True looks like he is going to steal one more bicycle from the neighborhood today evening when it turns dark. Let us catch him red-handed!"

Chapter 4: The Final Confrontation

The four friends were super excited as they were near to catching the thief.

They all gathered opposite the fourth address and hid behind the bush.

Olivia: (whispering) "Let us hide hear and wait for the thief and when he attempts to steal the bicycle, we will catch him red-handed."

The team waited for some time until it turned dark. After some time a van came and parked in front of the house.

A tall dark person wearing a cap and glasses got down and started acting suspiciously near a bicycle rack.

Lily: (whispering) "Look, someone, is acting suspiciously near the bicycle rack. Could it be the thief?"

Leo: (observing the suspect) "He is wearing a cap and dark glasses, trying to hide his identity. He must be the thief."

Olivia: (determined) "Let's gather more evidence before we confront them. We need to be sure."

After some time the man lifted the bicycle parked in the rack and started putting it in the back of his van.

Max: (whispering) "Look he is stealing the bicycle. Now is the right time to catch him. Let's go!"

Max, Olivia, Leo, and Lily ran towards the thief. Leo started blowing his whistle to make a large sound and gather people from the neighborhood.

Max: (firmly) "We know you've been stealing bicycles, and we have the proof. Confess now!"

The suspect was taken aback by the sudden attack of detective friends.

Suspect: (startled) "I... I didn't do.."

Leo: (firmly) "We have all the evidence against you. We know your hiding place in the old shed."

Meanwhile, people from the neighborhood came out to see what the sound was about.

Suspect: (shivering on seeing the crowd) "I mean.. I... Ok, I did it, but it's personal, okay? I had my reasons."

"These boys made a lot of noise when they were playing and I could not concentrate because of their sounds"

Olivia: (compassionately)
"We understand you had your grievances, but stealing isn't the solution. You need to make things right."

Leo: (calmly) "We recovered the stolen bikes. It's time to return them to their rightful owners."

Lily: (supportive) "Let's learn from this experience and find better ways to resolve our issues."

Later the team took the bicycle owners to the shed and returned their bicycles. The crowd took the suspect and handed him to the police.

Chapter 5: The Thanksgiving

Thomas: "I am so thankful to you guys for coming here and sorting out this bicycle mystery."

Sam: "Myself and Emma did not even call you, yet you were so humble to approach us and give back our missing bicycles."

Emma: "Exactly Thanks a lot. You are our favorite Detective Friends!"

Neighbor: "You kids are amazing! You've shown true bravery and detective skills. Thank you for bringing justice to our community."

Max: (grateful) "We couldn't have done it without each other. Our friendship and determination led us to the truth."

Olivia: (smiling) "And we'll continue solving mysteries together, making sure our neighborhood stays safe."

Leo: (nodding) "Absolutely. We've shown everyone that we can make a difference when we work together."

Lily: (inspired) "And we've also learned that there's always a better way to solve problems, without resorting to theft."

Max, Olivia, Leo, and Lily, together with their newfound friends, form a neighborhood watch group to ensure the safety and well-being of their community.

6. The Mystery of the Disappearing Books

In the quiet town of Willowbrook, the local library was a hub of knowledge and imagination. Children would visit the library and stay there for hours reading books.

Chapter 1: The Library's Lament

Daniel was a super enthusiastic kid, who would spend most of his time in the library. One day when he was reading a book in the library, his friends approached him.

George: (with football in his hand) "There you are my friend Daniel. I knew that you would be sitting here in the library. We are going out to play a game of football. So come and join us."

Daniel: "No guys you go and play. I want to finish this book. It is very interesting."

Andrew: (convincing Daniel) "Oh come on my friend, play with us and I am sure you will have lots of fun."

Daniel: (denying) "No guys, I am middle of a very interesting chapter of this book and I want to finish it, you guys can go and play."

Andrew and George were disappointed and left Daniel in the library.

Daniel continued to enjoy reading the books in the library. Everything was going perfectly until strange things started happening in the library.

Books were mysteriously vanishing from the shelves and many of the books started to have missing pages.

Olivia was also a member of this library and when she came to know about these mysteries, she approached the librarian, Ms. Thompson, "Good Afternoon Mam! I heard rumors that books have started disappearing in this library. Is that correct?"

Ms Thompson: (concerned) "yes my dear. We are finding that a lot of books have gone missing from the rack recently."

"Also, we found that many of the books were having their pages missing. We are trying hard to find the culprit, but we are not able to get any clues about it."

Olivia: (consoling) "Please do not worry mam. I and my friends can help you find the culprit. We often take such small detective tasks to help people. Would you like us to investigate this matter?"

Ms Thompson: (grateful) "I appreciate your enthusiasm, and we would be grateful if you can help us sort things back."

Olivia: (excited) "Thank you mam for providing us with this opportunity. We will surely find the culprit and bring him to you."

Chapter 2: The Investigation

Olivia called an emergency meeting and soon Max, Leo and Lily were in the library to discuss the new mystery.

Olivia: (taking the lead) "Dear friends our favorite library is under threat. Someone is stealing and tempering the books here."

Lily: (scared) "Oh that's terrible. Why would someone damage the library? Could it be some ghosts coming out in the night and causing this?"

Leo: (joking) "Yes why not? Ghosts like to eat books! That's their favorite food!"

Olivia: (annoyed) "Leo you and your jokes!"

Leo: (joking) "Or even better, it looks like Library had hurt someone and so that guy is taking revenge and destroying books!"

Max: (eating chocolate cookie) "Enough Leo. Dear friends let us put on our detective hats and solve this case. This is a high-priority case as the library is public property and we cannot let anyone damage the public property. Let us all form a team and investigate this case."

The detective friends began their investigation, carefully examining the empty spaces on the shelves. Since the library was a two-storeyed building, they decided to split up into teams and keep a watch on the library.

Max: "I and Olivia will keep a watch on the ground floor and Lily and Leo you go and keep a watch on the upper floor."

Lily: "OK friends let us keep a watch.
The friends kept a close watch on everyone for the entire day but nothing happened. So they got together in the evening."

Lily: "Friends I think the culprit is smart enough and will not come in the daytime when there are people around."

Max: "True, the culprit is very smart. Must be coming in the nighttime to damage the books."

Olivia: "Look friends I have taken the keys and permission from Ms Thompson to stay back in the library. We can stay back here after the library closes and observe it."

Lily: (scared) "Are we sure there are no ghosts at nighttime here?"

Leo: (scaring her) "Of course yes. I already told them, they come out at night to eat the books."

Olivia: (consoling) "Do not worry. We are all together here. So nothing to worry about. Let us all inform our home that we will be coming back a bit late tonight."

Chapter 3: The Literary Culprit

All four friends informed their parents that they will be spending some more time in the library. As it turned dark, the detective friends again spread out to keep watching on both floors of the library.

After waiting for half an hour, then suddenly heard a voice near the stairs of the library.

Max: (whispering) "See Olivia, someone is here."

Olivia: (carefully watching) "I don't think he is very big. Looks like a child like us. Let us follow him."

Max and Olivia carefully and quietly follow the boy.

On the other hand, Lily observed someone on the first floor and whispered, Leo see someone is here. Let us follow him.

Lily and Leo followed the second culprit and observed him from a distance.

Leo: (whispering) "See Lily he is tearing the pages from the book. I think we have caught the culprit."

Lily: (confirming) "True Leo, let's call our friends and catch him red-handed."

Leo and Lily quietly went down the stairs to call Max and Olivia. Max and Olivia were hiding behind a rack and observing someone.

Olivia: (whispering) "See Max, that child is stealing the books and putting them in his bag. We have our culprit."

Max: (confirming) "yes here we have our thief. Let us catch him."

Meanwhile Lily and Leo also join them.

Lily: (scared) "If the thief is here, we also saw someone upstairs tearing pages from books."

Leo: (wondering) "I think it is a gang of thieves. We need to catch them all."

Olivia: "True friends let us catch them before they escape."

Chapter 4: Unmasking the Thieves

Max: (firmly) "Stop right there, we have caught you. We know that you are stealing books here and we know that you have someone helping you upstairs."

Olivia turned on the library lights and they realized that it was one of their school friends George.

George: (scared) "No stop. I am not a thief. Please stop!"

On hearing this sound, the culprit on the upper floor came down to see what was happening.

The detective friends looked towards the stairs and realized that it was their other school friend Andrew.

Leo: (loudly) "George and Andrew why are you guys stealing and damaging library books? Tell us or we will call the police."

Andrew: (scared) "No no please don't tell anyone. We are not doing it for us, we are doing it for our friend Daniel."

Max: (surprised) "What Daniel is responsible for all this? I thought he loved the library."

"He lives nearby let me call him before we discuss it further."

Olivia: "And I will go and call Ms Thompson."

In a few moments, Ms. Thompson and Daniel came along with a few parents and neighbors.

Daniel: (shocked) "My friends Andrew and George! Max told me that I asked you to damage the library. When did I tell you to do so? I love the Library so much!"

George: "Yes exactly! You love it so much that you have become a bookworm and are not coming out to play with your friends."

Andrew: "True. We come to call you several times but you are never interested in any sports."

"All you care about is your books. And apart from that you are not at all interested in any sports or friends."

"We care for you and so we decided to take you away from this library by removing the books that you like to read."

Olivia: (consoling) "Andrew and George your intentions are very good, but what you have done is not correct. The library is public property. The books in the library are read not only by Daniel but by several other kids also.

Ms Thompson: "Certainly. You can't damage the library to get Daniel out of the library. And Daniel it is also your fault. While you read the books, you must also spend time with your friends and in sports."

Daniel: (shameful) "I am sorry Ms Thompson. I realize my mistake. Oh my dear friends I am so sorry for hurting your sentiments. I am really lucky to have such caring friends."

All three friends hug each other.

Andrew: "We are really sorry for what we have done."

"We will return all the books that we stole from the library."

George: "Please forgive us. We will also repair the books that we have damaged. "

"Please forgive us, please.. please.."

Ms. Thomspon: "It is okay my dear children. I am also thankful to the four detective friends for staying back so late and solving this case."

"Now go back to your home and come tomorrow to restore the books."

Max: "On that note, let us now all go back to our homes. I am already very hungry and my stomach is crying for some food."

Leo: (joking) "I am sorry but I cannot hear your stomach crying. Can you ask it to cry a little louder?"

Olivia: (laughing) "Oh Leo you and your jokes!"

That night everyone went back to their homes with a smile on their face. The next day Ms Thompson along with George, Daniel, and Andrew restored the books and Library was back to its normal shape.

THE END

7. The Mystery at the Amusement Park

After a long wait, the beloved amusement park Thrillville was reopened for the residents of Fairview City.

The park had undergone a major renovation and a whole new bunch of rides had been added.

Some of these rides included crazy and scary roller coaster rides. Everyone was super excited to see these rides and experience the thrill of sitting on these rides.

Chapter 1: A Day of Adventure

Just after two days after opening, a series of mishappenings began inside this amusement park.

The rides would suddenly halt in the middle, some of the rides would not start at all, and some of the rides would make very loud annoying noises when they were operated.

Everyone was disappointed by these developments and slowly the crowd started to turn away from the amusement park.

The owner of the park Mr. James, was very upset with these events. He asked his staff members to carefully examine every ride and make sure that these events do not happen again. Yet every morning they found that one or two rides would misbehave.

Max's father (Mr. Jones) was a close friend of Mr James. So when he heard the news about the amusement park, he took Max and his detective friends to the Amusement park to meet Mr. James.

Jones: (cheerfully) "Ah there you are my friend James. How are you? How are things going here?"

James: (depressed) "Oh my dear friend Jones. So glad to see you. I am good, but something is not right with the park."

Jones: (nodding) "I heard some rumors about the strange happenings in this park. Is it true?"

James: "Unfortunately yes my friend. Every day some ride here seem to misbehave. Looks like something is fishy here."

Jones: (consoling) "Don't you worry my friend. Let me introduce you to my son Max and his three friends. These guys are good at solving such mysteries and recently have solved many such cases."

James: (with a new spark in his eyes) "Oh really! Hello Max. I need your help. Can you help me restore my park?"

Max: "Certainly. Let me introduce you to my friends Olivia, Leo, and Lily."

"Together we are a great detective team and we will try our level best to crack this case."

Olivia: (consoling) "Please don't worry Mr James. We will surely find the culprit for you."

Chapter 2: The Roller Coaster Mishap

Mr. James took the detective friends to show them the park's newest roller coaster, Thunderbolt.

Mr. James: "This is an amazing ride. Brand new and recently assembled. Even this ride started misbehaving and had we not stopped this ride on time, there would have been a major mishap."

"Luckily our operator was quick enough to sense the abnormal sound coming from this ride and he immediately stopped the ride."

Max: "Please allow us to inspect this site. We would like to look for clues at this place."

James: "Surely, please feel free to have a look around. I will instruct my staff to cooperate with you. Meanwhile, I and Jones will head to my office in this park for a cup of coffee."

James took Jones to his cabin and asked his staff to help the detective friends.

Max: (grabbing a bite of his favorite cookie) "Okay my detective friends. It is time to put on our detective hats and solve this puzzle."

Olivia: (observing) "There are so many people here in the Amusement park and it is so large, it is very difficult to track suspects here."

Lily: (scared) "What if someone ghostly figure comes in the night and damages the rides? Do you guys think there is such a possibility?"

Leo: (joking) "100%. I fully agree with Lily. It could be the work of some ghost who lives here and does not like the exciting noises made here by children while riding the roller coaster. Max let us ask Mr James to leave this haunted place!"

Olivia: (annoyed) "Shut up Leo. And Lily have you ever seen a ghost? Then why are you always so scared?"

Lily: (explaining) "Exactly Olivia I have never seen a ghost and that is what scares me! I wonder how dangerous it might be!"

Max: (leading) "Enough of talk friends. Let us get into some action. I and Olivia will make some inquiries about the roller coaster. Leo and Lily, you can go to the other side of the park near the Pendulum rides, where people were reporting annoying noise when Pendulum moved."

Leo: (agreeing) "Copy that Max."

As per the plan, the detective friends split up and started independent investigations in different areas of the Park.

Chapter 3: The Investigation

Leo went and asked the employees around the ride if they had noticed anything suspicious.

After some time Leo came back and said: "I just now inquired the staff. They informed me that yesterday someone had removed the entire grease from the ball bearings of this pendulum ride, which resulted in a large annoying sound when it operated."

Lily: (observing) "Leo can you see those that rag near the corner of the Pendulum ride? I think it is full of grease."

Leo: "Yes it is a dirty rag. It must have been used to remove the grease."

Lily: "I think the culprit must have some traces of grease left over on him. Let us try to observe people nearby to see if we can spot anything."

Leo and Lily started observing the people in the park from a distance.

Meanwhile, Max and Olivia finished inquiring the employees about the roller coaster.

Max: "Olivia the employees pointed out that someone had fiddled with the screws of the tracks on the roller coaster."

Olivia: (thinking) "It looks like it has to be the work of a technician because ordinary people can't do such technical stuff."

Max: (confirming) "True. Let's watch out if we can find any suspicious technician out here."

Chapter 4: The Revelation

All four detective friends met again to discuss their findings.

Lily: "Our findings reveal that the culprit should have some grease stains on him."

Olivia: "And we found that it has to be the work of a technician, who understands the details of the rides."

Max: "Alright friends so it looks like we now know what the culprit should look like."

"Now let us go and see if we can find anyone with similar traits"

Leo: "Surely he should be here planning his next move, so better catch him before he damages one more ride."

All the detective friends spread out in the park to see if they can find their suspect.

Max, Olivia, and Leo struggled to find the culprit.

But Lily with her sharp observation skills was confident that she should be able to spot him from a distance. After spending some time, she noticed that a tall person was curiously looking at a ride.

Lily looked at his shoes and immediately realised that they were having stains of grease.

Lily's suspicion grew as he kept hopping around from one ride to another, without actually getting on the rides.

She quickly called all her friends along with Mr James and Mr Jones.

Lily: "See that tall guy carefully. His shoes have stains of grease and he is acting suspiciously."

Mr James: (identifying) "Oh that guy looks like Stewart, our technician whom we fired for his misconduct before we closed the park for renovation."

Max: "If he is a technician, he must be knowing about all the technical aspects of these rides."

Olivia: "Certainly he is watching those rides carefully as if he is planning something."

Mr Jones: "James I think we should have an investigation with him."

Mr James: "Certainly. Let me call him. Hey Stewart, how come you are here?"

Stewart: (baffled) "Oh Mr. James. I just came to see the park."

Max: May "I ask you why you have grease on your shoes Mr.?"

Stewart: (scared) "Oh it is just from my workshop. It has nothing to do with the Pendulum ride."

Max: (smiling) "But I never said anything about the Pendulum ride."

"How did you know that someone wiped off all grease from the Pendulum ride?" Max asked to Stewart."

Stewart: (scared – on being caught) "I..I. don't know what you are talking about."

Mr. James: "I know you, Stewart."

"Your behavior was not good earlier also and that is why I fired you. I think that it is you who is causing this mischief in my park."

On being exposed, Stewart started running towards the gate. Mr. James asked his security to catch hold of him. The security standing at the gate caught Stewart who was trying to run out of the gate.

James: "You should be ashamed of yourself. Because you grudge me, you are putting the lives of innocent people in danger. I will not tolerate this. I am going to call the police."

Chapter 5: A Park Reborn

Soon the police came down to the park and on seeing the police, Stewart confessed his offense.

With the culprit caught, Thrillville was saved from closure.

Mr. James got all the damaged rides inspected and corrected.

On hearing the news of the culprit being caught, the residents of Fairview gathered in the park to show their support for the park.

Mr. James: "My dear friends. I am happy to announce that with the help of the four detective friends Max, Olivia, Leo, and Lily we have been able to catch the culprit who was causing the mischief with rides."

"Now all the rides are safe and there is nothing to worry about."

"On this occasion I am happy to offer free rides to every one of you gathered here for today."

"So feel free to explore your favorite ride today."

The crowd hailed in joy. Especially the children were very happy and super excited.

Mr. James: (thanking) "My friend Jones thank you so much for coming and bringing these brilliant kids who help us restore our park."

Mr. Jones: "No worries at all. No need to thank the kids after all it is their favorite destination too!"

Max: "Exactly. The culprit was playing with our favorite park and the Pendulum wheel is one of my favorite rides. How can we let someone damage it."

Leo: "In fact, we would like to thank you for offering free rides today. I am super excited to sit on my favorite rides."

Lily: "Exactly Thank you, Mr James."

Max: "Come on friends let us explore the new rides in the park. Can't wait to sit in my favorite rides."

That day all the kids including the detective friends had a fun time at the park, where they enjoyed their favourite rides. Finally, Thrillville thrived once again, bringing joy and excitement to visitors of all ages.

THE END

Did you enjoy reading this book?
Are you ready to witness more thrilling adventures of our detective friends?

The world is full of mysteries waiting to be solved, and your imagination and keen eye can unlock endless possibilities.

Keep exploring, keep solving, and always trust in the power of your curiosity. And if you liked this book and want to stay updated with the next book in this series, then ask someone senior to subscribe to our email list by clicking here https://ujbbooks.com/unityb/
Until our next thrilling adventure, stay curious and never stop seeking the truth. Goodbye for now!

Please take a moment to share your thoughts and feedback.

 www.facebook.com/ujbbooks

 www.instagram.com/ujbbooks

 editor@ujbbooks.com

Printed in Great Britain
by Amazon